Lady Scarlett
A Retelling of The Highwayman

M.K. Felix

Cover by: GetCovers

eBook ISBN: 979-8-9931091-3-8

Paperback ISBN: 979-8-9931091-4-5

Contents

For my beta readers.

My stories wouldn't be what they are without you. Thanks for making sure

I do my characters justice.

This one is for you, my biggest fans and cheerleaders.

Warning

WARNING

Dear Reader,

Lady Scarlett is best read after *Fairest Hunter*. *Lady Scarlett* is a companion novella, focusing on two side characters from *Fairest Hunter*. Some scenes overlap between the two books, and you'll see the same characters make appearances.

In an effort to not spoil the climax of *Fairest Hunter*, I have purposefully left details more vague in *Lady Scarlett* and focused on the relationship between William and Marian instead.

All this to say, if you read this novella before *Fairest Hunter*, the key points of that story will, for the most part, be a surprise to you. If you read *Lady Scarlett* afterward, you'll get more behind the scenes from the fan-favorite side characters.

Either way, I did my best to make this story as standalone as possible, while occurring at the same time as *Fairest Hunter*.

Enjoy,

M.K. Felix

Prologue

Lady Marian Wessex

My pale-pink dress is at odds with my dour mood. Though there isn't anything I can do about the color, seeing as King Ferdinand forbade us from wearing mourning blacks for Prince Alvor, I don't have to smile.

The desire to smile is nonexistent today. Nothing about this gathering at the king's castle encourages me to feel anything but contempt and sadness.

The young men around me are sniveling, the women are simpering, and it all feels like too much. I haven't even heard the king speak yet, but I know it'll just make today worse. I always leave the castle morose, and spending time here makes it hard to think. I'm blaming it on the overly perfumed women and the choking colognes the men wear.

The doors of the ballroom are thrown open, and in waltzes King Ferdinand, a monstrous golden crown atop his head and red robes with golden trim and lace covering every inch of the fabric.

It's gaudy, and I hate it.

The room falls silent, and the buzzing in my mind quiets, only to be replaced by a thick fog as King Ferdinand speaks.

"My friends. I appreciate all who have expressed their condolences at the loss of my son. It is truly . . . tragic."

It really is tragic. Prince Alvor was the only kind man in the courts.

My nose starts to tingle as my eyes sting.

"Seeing as I no longer have an heir, it is time for me to remarry. Our kingdom has been without a queen for too long. Which is why I will be choosing a bride from among the nobility of our people."

The rest of King Ferdinand's words flow past my ears without me hearing them.

A bride from among the nobility.

That could be me.

My stomach churns, and I lift my hand to cover my mouth.

Quiet clapping sounds around me, and though I don't know what we're clapping for, I reluctantly join in.

"As we are to soon have a series of balls as I find my future wife, I will dismiss you all. Do not forget to settle your accounts with my steward as you leave today."

Heads bob as the sea of nobility exits the ballroom, not a complaint that we came here for a simple announcement among them.

Father grips my arm tightly. "We must hurry, Marian."

"Why?" I ask.

He shakes his head, frantically looking around him. "I will speak of it later. For now, let us leave."

My brows furrow, but I keep my complaints and questions to myself.

We're ushered out of the castle after Father pays his gold coin for attending the function. It's a recent change that King Ferdinand instated, citing it necessary to pay for the lavish parties he throws for his nobles. The party we didn't even get to participate in tonight.

Father ushers me into the carriage, and when the door closes, he lets out a heavy breath. He wipes his forehead with his handkerchief and watches the window with apprehension.

"What's wrong?" I ask.

Father takes a deep breath. "I've arranged for you to marry Prince Caladen of Rovia."

My jaw drops. "You have done *what*?"

Father keeps his gaze trained on the window. "It's a good thing, too. I do not wish you to be among the potential brides for King Ferdinand. When we get home, you shall pack up your things and I shall gather your dowry items. We'll head for the border tomorrow. We should arrive in Rovia the following day."

"But I don't even know him—"

Father's eyes turn on me. "No, but you shall do as you're told. It's for the best."

I bite my tongue. How many times have we attended court functions because it's "for the best"? I don't entirely trust that sentiment, especially when it takes a decision out of my hands.

If only I could escape all of this and choose a husband for myself.

Chapter One
An Indignant Lady

Lady Marian Wessex

I stare out the window of our carriage, unwilling to talk to Father, let alone look at him.

The trees are more entertaining, what with their majestic height. A flash of brown moves through the leaves, but I lose sight of it as we continue on the worn dirt road.

Father should be able to afford more comfortable carriages. We're to travel all the way to Rovia, and unfortunately my desire to not feel every hole or bump in the road will be unmet. My fingers clench in my lap. Marrying Prince Caladen of Rovia has never been a part of my plan for my life. Also, something must be wrong with him if he's willing to marry the daughter of a duke in a neighboring kingdom. He has princesses from other kingdoms to choose from, yet he's willing to settle for me?

Nope. Something must be wrong with him. Could I make a marriage to a stranger work? Yes. But I'd rather not.

My fingers play with the lace trim on my dress. I brush off a spot of dust on my lap. If only it was that easy to brush away the feelings of grief and confusion plaguing my mind.

Prince Alvor is dead, and though I wasn't in love with him, he was never unkind to me. I had hoped we could have even become friends one day. Now there is no chance of finding a kind suitor in Lyriva; maybe that's why Father has us traveling to Rovia. With Prince Alvor's death . . . there's no one left for me that qualifies as good enough in Father's eyes.

Father's feet tap impatiently against the floor of the carriage. "Marian . . ." he whines.

My nose presses against the glass as I shift as far away from Father as possible. The carriage jolts, and I stumble forward as we come to a halt.

"What is going on out there?" Father mutters.

I bite my tongue, holding in the sassy retort that would point out the obvious.

The unfamiliar voices from outside draw me to the carriage door, and my fingers brush the handle.

"Don't you dare open that door, Marian," Father scolds. "I will take care of this."

My eyes roll to the ceiling of the carriage. Yet, I'm a dutiful daughter, so I lean back and let Father scoot past me to exit the carriage.

He pushes the door open with enough force that the frame swings back and hits the carriage, making the glass rattle in its setting. The bellowing voice Father uses when most upset greets those on the other side of the small four walls I'm trapped within. "Excuse me. What is going on here? Do you not know who you have stopped?"

I pinch the bridge of my nose. *Ugh, the pompous attitude? Really, Father? You're a duke, but that doesn't change the fact that we're probably being held up by bandits.*

My hand drops from my face as I go back to watching Father and stopping myself from stepping down onto the dirt road to knock some sense into him before a bandit does. Father moves farther away from the carriage, and I keep my hand on the door, holding it open so I can hear more clearly what is being said.

"...All I have in my carriage is my daughter's dowry," Father states.

I can't hear what the bandit says, but when Father sputters again, I can't help but cover my smile. He's really selling this capable duke role, and again I wonder what he's going to do when I'm not here to help him navigate court life. I'm no expert, but Father only understands his ledgers, not the intricacies of relationships—something I've been studying since he brought me to court two years ago.

Father shouts, "You cannot. She is off to marry the prince of Rovia. You would dare endanger such a beneficial political alliance for our kingdom?"

Somebody gag me. I don't want to marry for an alliance. And I don't want to leave Lyriva either.

The bandit speaks, loud enough this time for me to hear. The tone of his voice intrigues me. "Then your daughter is welcome to marry one of my merry men, for today we are taking her dowry. You may relinquish it quietly and with ease, or we may tie you up and force you to hand over the dowry."

I don't hear what's said next as my mind races like one of Father's prized horses.

Rumors of Robin Hood and his merry men have infiltrated the court, many other noblemen having been robbed while riding the highways of the kingdom. There have also been whispers from the servants of poor, hungry families leaving for the woods and never returning from Sherwood Forest.

Maybe that's where all the good men have gone. They've turned into honorable outlaws who use their coins to quietly help the poor.

I'd be happy to marry an honorable outlaw who steals from the rich to feed the poor. He'd be better than the spineless boys of the court, because without Prince Alvor, there are no good noblemen left.

"She's going to be a princess!" Father shouts, his voice halting my contemplation.

Those words? They're the last straw.

I clench my teeth as I sit up, gripping the silk folds of my skirt in a tight fist as I throw the carriage door open. The glass panes don't rattle this time.

My calf-skin boots hit the dirt and I turn, staring down the men even as I smooth my skirts. I step toward Father, who's surrounded by hooded men dressed in leather and looking like they're part of the forest.

They're also holding weapons.

I force myself to take a deep breath through the tightness in my chest. I focus on Father and stare into his wide eyes. "I told you I do not want to marry Rovia's prince, Father. But you didn't listen to me. Take this as the sign it is—that I will not marry a man I have never met. No matter if it makes me a princess. I do not care for them. I'd rather marry one of these bandits, for at least they have honor, unlike you—riding away without telling a soul where I'm going. And for what? So you can avoid the king's suspicions? You don't even care that I'm heartbroken over Prince Alvor. So no. I will not leave Lyriva."

I can't help it. I stomp my foot, even though I know it makes me look like a child. But I am so tired of Father choosing things for me. Forcing me to be at court. Matchmaking me with rude noblemen, and now deciding I'm going to marry a prince.

I. Don't. Want. A. Prince.

There's clapping.

Why is there clapping?

My gaze shoots to the man who I assume is the ringleader of these bandits. He stands before Father, clapping as he stares at me through his mask.

Father turns to the bandit. "What are you doing?"

The man continues his applause. "Celebrating a woman who knows her mind, and who has the guts to speak it. You'd do well to listen to her, for she'll guide you well."

Heat floods my cheeks, and I stare at the ground. Then I realize what he has said, and I straighten my spine. I move my shoulders back and raise my chin, holding myself as the lady my governess taught me to be.

The man in the hood, who I'd bet my dowry is Robin Hood, moves until I can see him fully. "My lady, if you ever wish to fall in love with a man who will respect your opinions and feelings, I offer you any of my merry men. They would do well to have a woman with such spirit at their side."

My eyes rove over this bandit. Something about the way he stands is different, and he doesn't speak like any man I know. No man has ever guessed my dreams, let alone something I decided I wanted less than a minute ago. A stray curl falls against my face, and I brush it away before looking around. The bandits are masked, but they have handsome facial structures. One melts from the forest, and though he's hooded, a red curl falls across his forehead.

His hair reminds me of my friend Elisabeth, whose locks match that color. The set of the man's shoulders reminds me of her older brother, long dead, though I don't doubt he'd have just as broad shoulders and handsome facial features if he were a bandit.

Resolve grows within me.

"See, Father? These men understand me. So it's either me or the dowry. Give them the money, and I'll go home and choose who I want to marry from the local nobleman. Or, keep the money, and I'll run away with these bandits."

It's a trap, one I should feel bad for using, but after studying books on warfare, and learning the art of twisting my words from the court, what does he expect? I know my father, and there is no way the illustrious Duke Wessex will settle for a lowly nobleman as my future husband—not when he's lost the chance for me to wed a prince. Which means I'll get my pick from these fine bandits.

Maybe I should call them highwaymen instead of bandits. Sounds more romantic that way.

I'm startled when Robin Hood bows. "My lady. I'd be happy to send any of my men to marry you at your own home. I'm afraid the woods would be no place for a fine young woman with tender sensibilities."

My hands land on my hips, and I glare at this ridiculous man. "What happened to me knowing my own mind?" Anger simmers within me. "You know what. Forget it. I choose banditry."

I step toward the man with the shocking red hair peeking out from his hood and mask and loop my arm through his. "Come on, bandit. We're leaving."

My heeled boots stomp in the dirt as I pull the bandit with me into the trees without looking back.

Will I miss Father? Yes.

But what did he expect? Probably not for me to race into the forest with an unknown man.

But a girl can only take so much of court drama and a controlling, overprotective father. Sometimes she just wants an adventure and to fall in love with a highwayman.

CHAPTER TWO
An Enraptured Highwayman

William Scarlett

Duke Wessex I'm familiar with, but the woman flouncing through the forest in her scarlet dress while clinging to my arm . . . well, I can't place her or recall her name. She's familiar, but it's been so long since I was at court. She might have been too young to be introduced when I was last at the castle anyway. The woman looks to be about the age of my sister Elisabeth—freshly eighteen.

I clear my throat. "May I have the honor of knowing who it is I am escorting to our camp?"

The woman titters, her dark eyes flashing up to meet mine. "Oh, dear me. I haven't even introduced myself. I'm Lady Marian Wessex, daughter of the Duke of Wessex. And what should I call you? A bandit? A highwayman?"

She *is* one of Elisabeth's friends. Memories of avoiding the two young girls flash in my mind. I'd avoid her visits, as there was no patience in my young self to deal with young girls who giggled more than spoke. There seems to be that same naivety about her even now, her smile seemingly untouched by the darkness of the king's curse.

But who knows how my sister has changed since my faked death? Maybe Lady Marian has changed too and this unguarded smile masks hidden depths. I'm sure she has not come out of the court unscathed by the greed of the king, and depravity of the unchecked noblemen.

Lady Marian smiles as she walks through the woods, taking in her surroundings with childlike wonder. I haven't been around someone so joyful in years. The energy coursing through this young woman is contagious, and I find myself smiling as I look down at her.

Now, what name should I give her?

My full name? No.

My given name? Nope. Not yet, at least.

I settle on the nickname I've heard daily over the last three years. "Red."

Lady Marian's nose wrinkles. "I can't call you Red. That's a color, not a name."

I shrug. "Sure it is."

Lady Marian stops and tugs on my arm with a surprising amount of force. I plant my feet, turning toward her.

She glares at me, her lips set in a pout. "No. I will not stand for it. You deserve a better name than Red. Something more noble, more romantic."

Something about the way Lady Marian waves her hand in the air with the word *romantic* has my mischievous side coming out to play. That teasing I usually reserve for my sisters or Robin creeps forward, and I find myself voicing the preposterous idea flitting through my head before I have time to think it through. "What would you trade me for my name?"

Her dark brows arch, her eyes widening as her petite mouth opens, gaping at me. "Trade you? Is it not enough that you and your men have already taken my dowry?"

I shrug. "What use have I for coins when I live off of the land? When the forest provides me with all I need? Trade me something of worth and I'll tell you my name, Lady Marian."

Her mouth snaps shut, her lips pursing, emphasizing their raspberry color as she studies my face. I haven't been this fascinated by a pair of lips in years. At first, I was captivated by the mystery of Lady Marian, but now, her wit and the glow of her humor have me entranced. I cautioned Robin, our fearless leader who happens to be a woman, about falling for Prince Alvor, who we recently saved. But I can't help that my heart is beating double time as I stare at the beautiful woman before me.

What I first thought was a naïve innocence in her eyes now reveals itself as scheming mischief. There's intelligence in this woman's face, from the way her eyes pierce mine to her folded arms and straight back.

Confidence looks good on Lady Marian.

She takes a small step closer to me, her voice dropping from a soprano to a mesmerizing alto. "Look here, highwayman. I may be a lady, but don't expect me to be clueless. I just abandoned my life five minutes ago to live in a forest with a group of strangers. So if you think I'm going to let you play around with me, you're mistaken. I will find out your name one way or another, and if you don't have the decency to share it with me, then I won't have the decency to speak to you for the rest of this journey."

The fire in this woman heats me to my core.

I step back, executing a perfect bow, one that Mother had me practice to perfection when I was younger. When I straighten, those discerning dark eyes find mine and pierce through me until she sees more of me than anyone has in years.

"My apologies, m'lady. I'm afraid living with bandits has roughened me up, and I've quite forgotten my manners." I reach out and slip my hand beneath her palm, bringing her knuckles to my lips where I brush a kiss against her soft skin. "Forgive me?"

Lady Marian stills, her eyes trained on where her hand lingers an inch from my mouth, before she shakes her head and pulls her hand from my grasp. "Forgiveness must be earned, highwayman."

"And names have power, Lady Marian." I tilt my head, studying the blush on her cheeks. "So I ask, what would you trade to know my name?"

She chews on her bottom lip for a moment before that confidence infuses her once more. "Are you open to negotiations, highwayman?"

I can't help but smirk. "Would I be a good highwayman if I wasn't?"

Lady Marian tilts her head to match the angle of mine, her lips quirking up at the corners. "Seeing as you're the first highwayman I've met, I would say yes. But that'd be because this situation works in my favor."

I take a small step forward, amusement seeping into my voice. "Seeing as you're being honest with me, which is quite refreshing, I have to say that I am open for negotiations."

Lady Marian smiles, though there's a hint of wariness in her gaze. "Perfect. Then when we make the trade, I get to not only learn your full name, but also to see your face without the mask."

I arch my eyebrows. "When we make the trade?"

She wrings her hands, clasping them at her waist. "Yes, though you might think my trade is silly."

"If you find it valuable, then it is not silly. You've proven a worthy verbal opponent, and like Robin Hood said, you are a strong woman who knows her mind. You have my respect, Lady Marian."

She steps closer, and the scent of her floral perfume washes over me. "Then I wish to make a trade with you, highwayman." Her hands come up and rest against my chest, her touch featherlight. Her chin tilts up until I'm staring down into her beautiful brown eyes.

Instinctively I reach out, gripping her waist, steadying her as her skirts press up against my legs. My voice comes out as a whisper, the enchantment she's woven over me with her proximity stealing any chance of clear thought. "What do you wish to trade, my lady?"

Her hand comes up, snaking around my neck, her fingers weaving into my hair. She pulls my head down toward hers as she whispers, "A kiss."

CHAPTER THREE
A Mischievous Trade

Lady Marian Wessex

My highwayman stills in my arms, his lips a breath away from mine. "Are you sure?" he whispers, the words soothing my soul yet shattering the confidence I felt a moment before. My fingers untangle themselves from his hair, sliding down to his chest as I lean back and look up into his eyes framed by the black cloth tied around his head. He is achingly still, those blue eyes staring into mine as a stray curl of his red hair falls over his forehead.

I've yet to be kissed, and I think I've waited long enough. This highwayman is already more of a gentleman than any of the nobles I've interacted with at court. It's not like they've harmed anyone they've robbed, and if the rumors are true, they use the coin to help penniless villagers. Their intentions are noble, though illegal, and the respect I've received from this man as we've traveled in the forest is more than I've been granted from noblemen.

So what's the harm in kissing him?

It's just a kiss.

His heart pounds beneath my fingertips, a sure sign I'm not the only one feeling the tension between us. "I've chosen to marry a highwayman. Did you not hear me tell my father?"

It's as if my words have unlocked something inside him. My highwayman smirks and finally moves forward, his nose brushing against mine. "I thought you were joking, Marian."

A shiver travels down my spine from his use of my name. I shake my head just a fraction of an inch. When I can't stand the distance between our lips for one moment longer, I whisper, "Do you accept my trade, highwayman?"

"Yes," he murmurs.

My eyes close as soft lips touch mine, the brush of whiskers against my skin unfamiliar yet pleasant.

My mind is at once overwhelmed by the deluge of sensations, unsure of what to do or focus on. He smells of pine sap. His lips are soft in contrast to the coarseness of his whiskers. He holds me tightly yet with tenderness—a heady sensation.

When his lips pull away from mine, my heart tugs as if bereft without his touch.

His voice has dropped an octave, his breath brushing against my lips. "Will you kiss me back, Marian?"

My cheeks burn—the moment ruined as my stomach curdles. "I... I don't know how."

I duck my head and push against his chest to escape his hold. But instead of letting me go, he tugs me closer, wrapping his arm around my waist like an iron band.

"Then let me show you," he whispers. His hand cups my jaw, tilting my head toward him with a gentleness that has my heart aching.

I blink away the burning moisture in my eyes and suck in a breath as my highwayman leaves a trail of kisses from my cheek to my ear. "Don't overthink it," he whispers, sending a shiver up my spine. "Do what feels natural."

"Okay," I whisper on what little breath I have left as his mouth captures mine.

It's like a dance, a natural give and take, as his lips caress mine. My heart races, my body feeling as if it's soaring amongst the clouds as my highwayman kisses me with what I can only describe as gentle passion, one with which I try to reciprocate.

I feel beautiful, cherished, and like a princess as my highwayman holds me in his arms. In what seems like a lifetime later, but truly is only a few moments, he pulls back, chest heaving beneath my palms.

No words are said as we stare into each other's eyes. I study the bright blue of his irises, a stark contrast to the black cloth still covering his face.

"Well, my fair Lady Marian. Your trade was more than enough." His thumb caresses my cheek one last time before reaching behind his head and tugging off the mask around his face.

A familiar face greets me. A face I once had girlish fancies about.

Fancies and daydreams that died three years ago.

"William Scarlett?" I whisper before everything goes black.

There's an annoying pain in my back. I try to turn over because this pillow is uncomfortable. What sort of bed is this?

The smell hits me next. Dirt, trees, and something manly hits my nose.

My room does not smell like this.

A deep voice murmurs something, and it takes a moment before I distinguish my name.

"Marian," William Scarlett murmurs.

I blink away the fading darkness to see blue eyes staring at me.

"William?" I whisper, not quite believing what I'm seeing.

He grins sheepishly, his red curls bouncing as he tilts his head. "Yes, it's me. Didn't expect you to faint when I took off my mask, though."

I sit up on the forest floor, his arms wrapped around me falling away as I compose myself. I can't help but reach out and smack his chest as I glare at him. "What did you expect when I realized I was kissing a dead man?"

He shrugs, his eyes flashing with mischief. "More kissing?"

I smack his chest again. He winces as he rubs the sore spot. I don't let on that my fingers sting a little.

My eyes narrow even more until there's only a slit in which I can see the ridiculously handsome man. "Absolutely not. No more kissing for you. I need an explanation."

I fold my arms, determined not to move from this spot in the dirt and leaves until I know why my best friend's older brother is sitting in front of me when we've all thought he was long dead.

William sighs and stands up from his crouch. "You'll get one. Let me take you to camp. You can sit in an actual chair there."

I look down at my silk dress with its snags, the dirt lining the hem, and I try not to think about how the red fabric will look more brown after this adventure. Maybe the lace will still be salvageable. "Fine," I huff. "But only because I care about this dress."

He smirks, and I desperately want to slap that look off his face. Or maybe kiss it off.

Undecided at this point.

Oh. My. I just kissed William Scarlett. Elisabeth's older brother. A future duke of Lyriva.

And it was . . . quite enjoyable.

William holds out his hand for me, and I slip my fingers into it. He tugs me upright with barely any effort. He squeezes my hand before letting go, his fingers trailing against mine as he pulls away, a mischievous smile on his lips.

My heart races as my chest constricts.

What in the world have I gotten myself into?

CHAPTER FOUR
An Enlightening Magic

William Scarlett

Marian loops her arm through mine, and I try to clear away as many branches away from her as possible as we go through the thickest part of Sherwood Forest. It'll be a while before we'll make it back to camp, yet I haven't heard her complain, even though I know those boots she's wearing are more for decoration than practicality.

My heart hasn't stopped racing since Marian fainted in my arms and my magic leapt to the surface after lying dormant for years.

Nor can I get that kiss out of my mind.

Even though Much, one of my fellow merry men, teases me about being a ladies' man, I haven't found a woman I've liked enough to pursue, let alone kiss in recent years. I greatly admire the women in our camp who are strong, work hard, and have sacrificed much. I've thought about pursuing one or two of them, but after speaking with them more, there never seemed to be a spark.

But with Marian? Well, there's a bonfire burning in my chest.

Though I doubt she'll let me kiss her again anytime soon. Nothing like realizing the person you're embracing is someone you thought was dead. Probably should have thought that one through, but who has time to think about important things like the past when the present is so much more entertaining?

"Marian, listen..." I start.

She holds up her hand and shakes her head. "Nope. I'm mad at you. Give me a few moments and then you can explain."

I bob my head even as my stomach sinks. "Fair enough."

We're silent as I lead us down the slim deer trail. I move to walk ahead of her when the trail grows thin, but am stopped when Marian tugs on my arm. I halt immediately and turn to her.

Those expressive eyebrows of hers are pulled together, her lips tilted downward. I feel like a teenage boy again—probably because I haven't kissed a woman since then. But I need to focus.

Now that she knows who I am, everything is different. Now I'm not a man in a mask—I'm William Scarlett, and though it's been three years since I've acted the son of a duke, I haven't forgotten the expectations put upon my behavior from the title.

I've never wanted to put on the mask in my pocket more.

Her brown eyes meet mine, her expression smoothing into confident determination. "William. That kiss back there? It didn't happen. You're a future duke, and I just told my father I'm marrying a bandit. But also, I'm quite upset with you."

My eyebrows arch, but she continues with her rant, stepping closer to me as her nose wrinkles, fire growing in her eyes. "How dare you kiss me like *that*, fully knowing who I was? You're my best friend's older brother, and now you've made everything—" She stomps her foot, her hands fluttering as she struggles for words. She lets out a growl and pokes me in the chest. "You are a scoundrel, William Scarlett, and I don't know what you did to me, but I seem to be thinking more clearly now than I have in years. Something is going on in this forest, and I'm going to get to the bottom of it. So you can either help me or get out of my way. But there will be no more kissing. You need to earn back my trust and respect. Understand?"

Marian folds her arms.

My magic flares to life again, the little spark igniting in my chest. My magic thrives on loyalty and cuts through lies and deceit. The small part of my mind where the light makes itself at home brightens, and I can see Marian clearly in a way that only Solwain, the gifter of magic, can understand. It's not often that my magic awakens, but with Marian, it's fully alive.

Marian glows in my sight, and knowledge settles into my mind as if it's always been there. Marian is fiercely independent, gifted with intelligence, and has a loyal heart of gold. There is a noble purpose awaiting her in Solwain's plan for our kingdom.

My chest tightens as more knowledge distills on my soul. Everything Marian said is true. I *must* earn back her trust and respect. Solwain demands it. Marian is no mere woman, and she will be an integral piece of our plans to better the kingdom. She must be welcomed into our fold, our camp, our band of rebels.

My shoulders sag, my mind sobering as the light in my mind fades, leaving behind a knowledge I can never doubt. Just as in times past when my magic has revealed a piece of Solwain's knowledge, my life shifts. Everything in my mind rearranges, absorbing the gift I've been bestowed with.

Now I know how much I've messed up and just how important Marian is to me and to Solwain's plans. Though it wasn't me who initiated the kiss, I am the one who took it past that of an innocent peck on the lips.

I bow my head before meeting her eyes. "I apologize, Lady Marian. It was never my intention to hurt you. Deception has become a part of my life over the past three years, and I can see now how that has damaged your trust. I respect you immensely, and if you'll do me the honor, I would appreciate the opportunity to welcome you to Robin Hood's camp. Some secrets are not mine to share, but I can promise that I will reveal as many as I am able to you, in atonement for my deception."

Marian studies me for a long moment. "Apology accepted. But William . . . there is more to me than you know. I may play the part of a naïve young girl, but do not underestimate me."

After what my magic showed me, I could never. So, I bow my head again, hand across my heart. "Understood, m'lady."

She clasps her hands at her waist. "Good. Now that we understand each other, take me to this camp of yours."

The endless energy is back in her steps, her smile wide on her face again as she snaps twigs and makes a racket as she tramps through the forest behind me.

As my mind runs over the knowledge gifted to me by Solwain, I gather one last piece of understanding. Lady Marian is a cunning woman—one who I'm afraid has already absconded with my heart.

Chapter Five
A Befuddling Night

Lady Marian Wessex

The thatched roof above me is quite boring to stare at, but there's little else to look at in the hut I share with the other single females in Robin Hood's camp. The scratchy blanket is spread over my legs, and the thin pillow behind my head does little to soften the discomfort of sleeping here. The blanket is a precious commodity, and I feel bad even thinking of complaints because the other women in the hut don't have one.

Though I'm starting to suspect that my pillow originally belonged to a redheaded highwayman, because every time I turn my head, all I can smell is William Scarlett.

My mind flits about, not sure what thought to land on or where my feelings should dwell. It's been a long day, and my body aches as much as my mind does.

Is this what a rag feels like? Used over and over, then wrung out to dry? It's as if I've been scrubbed against a washboard all day. When we got back to camp, I learned that Prince Alvor is alive, that William and others who I thought had died are very much alive. It all has been ... a shock, to say the least.

Though the biggest surprise, or rather the one I'm most excited about, was when I figured out at dinner that Robin Hood is a woman whom Prince Alvor seems to be in love with. Though the Prince and his lady love would screech if they knew I discovered that Rowena is Robin Hood. They took great pains to try to keep me in the dark, but I easily put the pieces together.

What can I say? Avoiding unwanted suitors takes wit and skill. Reading between the lines is one of my favorite activities.

William is an interesting person to try to read. He's confident and teasing with his friends, but around me, there seems to be a quiet soberness about him. I didn't mind playing up the act of flirting with him at dinner tonight—Prince Alvor only knows me as a tittering flirt, so I played my part well.

But the part that wasn't an act? Kissing William in the woods.

My fingers come up to my mouth, brushing against my lips at the memory of our clandestine rendezvous. The experience is one that will not be repeated, even if it's unbelievably easy to pretend to flirt with William and be smitten with him.

Okay, it's not really pretend, but my whole life has turned upside down, and though I told Father I'd marry a bandit, I don't know what I'm actually going to do anymore.

I turn over, trying to get comfortable, but it's practically impossible.

It's official. I've been spoiled by my feathered mattress at home in my mansion. This combination of wood, ropes, and stuffed straw is not cutting it.

A moment later, the woman next to me starts snoring... obnoxiously.

I hold in a groan and gather up my blanket, wrapping it around my shoulders as I slip out of the door. A small fire a way off draws me closer. A teenage girl tends the flames, and I slump on the empty log across from her, leaning toward the heat that offers a small amount of relief from the cool summer night. Our mansion in the capital is warmer, or maybe that's just the memory of the tended fires and layers of blankets I keep on my bed.

But this blanket, well . . . it's not the same.

Nothing is the same, but will it ever be? I can't go back to my life before coming to Sherwood Forest, and the weight of that knowledge rests on my shoulders, an ache I can't ignore.

Soft footfalls sound behind me, and I'm not surprised when a whispered voice says my name. "Marian."

I turn to find the man who gets my heart racing despite my reservations stepping from the shadows and up to my log. William slips into the empty spot beside me, his eyes fixed on the teenager across the fire who glares at him.

I nudge his shoulder. "Isn't this the women's side of camp? Aren't men forbidden to be here?"

He nods. "Yes. So I was wondering if you'd go for a walk with me back to the cook fire at the center of camp. I may be an outlaw, but I don't want to break Robin's laws." He drops his voice so only I can hear. "And I'm pretty sure I'm about to be ratted out."

I hold in my snort. The young woman's glare could rival even Robin's. Robin, who is in fact a woman herself, would definitely be mad if she caught William here, or Red, as he's known by the merry men.

I mean, it's clever, considering he has red hair and the last name of Scarlett, but also it's low-hanging fruit for a nickname. Though I can't seem to come up with a better one.

I nod. "Fine. But only to save you from breaking more rules."

He grins. "Your sacrifice is appreciated."

He holds out his hand for me to help me stand. Then I loop my arm through his, soaking in his warmth as he guides us through the maze of trees. A large campfire with several log benches around it greets me. My body hums from William's proximity and his warmth, which I need to get away from if I'm going to keep my resolve not to fall for the man. He's my best friend's older brother, and though I thought he was cute growing up, it doesn't seem right to be falling for him while his family still believes he's dead.

I quicken my step as we get close, and it's only William's quick reflexes that catch me when I trip. He pulls me to his side, his other hand coming around to land on my waist as he steadies me.

"Careful there, m'lady," he murmurs.

Goosebumps race up my arms. Ridiculous things.

"I'm not your lady," I hiss as I step out of his embrace.

He mumbles a response, and I know I shouldn't get my hopes up, because I think he said "not yet," and believing that would be too much for me today.

The butterflies in my stomach flutter despite myself. My heart and mind are at war, which is why when he sits next to me on an empty log across the fire from another couple, I don't protest.

"How are you doing?" His voice is low, sincerity laced in his words, sending those butterflies fluttering again.

I tilt my head, studying the flames before us. "About as well as can be expected."

"Despite the surprises of the day, you didn't seem to mind taking the chance to play matchmaker," he teases, and I can't help but smile.

Anyone with two eyes can see how much Prince Alvor and Rowena are attracted to each other. It's not my fault I pointed it out at dinner. No wonder Alvor never gave me the time of day, not if he's been pining after Rowena. Though I don't much care about his feelings for me at this point—there's another man taking up residence in my mind despite my best efforts to not lend out the space.

I bump William's shoulder as I pull my blanket tighter around my shoulders. "Don't deny it. Those two are in love."

He raises his hands as if he's innocent. "I'm not saying anything."

I lean forward, propping my elbows on my knees as I revel in the warmth of the flames, though I turn my head to better see William's face. "I noticed. You don't mind teasing your cousin, but you're oddly tight-lipped with me, William Scarlett."

"I would say I'm actually loose-lipped with you, Lady Marian."

My cheeks burn, even as a curl of pleasure winds around my heart as I stare at his smirk. Despite my better judgment, I fall into flirting with him again. "I don't know, William. I'm having a hard time remembering the experience. There were so many other things that happened today that my mind seems to have forgotten entirely any knowledge I have of your lips."

With a stealth showcasing his highwayman tendencies, his hand moves, tucking my hair out of the way as his lips brush against the tip of my ear, tickling my skin. "I highly doubt that, m'lady. Your mind is a steel trap. I wouldn't be surprised if you've discovered all of our secrets tonight, though you pretend you know nothing. And that kiss? It's branded my soul, and I'm afraid if you were to grace me with another I'd be unable to do anything with my days other than follow you wherever you go as your humble servant."

The fire is too hot. This blanket? Too confining.

And William Scarlett?

He is utterly too tempting.

I struggle to regulate my breathing as I hide any physical evidence of how William's words affect me. But he doesn't stop there. His hand snakes out, grabbing mine, which lets the corner of the blanket between us fall away. He pulls my hand to his lips, placing a kiss on my knuckles before letting it go and tucking the blanket around my shoulders again.

But the sensation of his lips on my skin doesn't fade away even as he turns back to the fire, a pleased smile on his face.

I squeeze my hands together, the blanket between them as I struggle to find something to say. All words have been blown away from my mind by William's declaration, and I'm scrambling to come up with something to say to the alluring man beside me. It doesn't even have to be an elegant conversation redirection; it just needs to be something.

My eyes land on the empty cook's table, and my thoughts lead me back to what is really happening in this camp.

"Let me help with your coup," I blurt out.

William stills, then chuckles. "Like I said—all of our secrets."

I shake my head, lowering my voice so only he can hear me. "You have the crown prince in your camp, there are rumors of curses, and Alvor's face was entirely too upset when he learned his father announced him dead and that his father wants to remarry and have another heir. Do you really expect me not to put it together that you're coming up with a plan to put Alvor on the throne?"

William shakes his head, a wry grin on his face. "I expected it, though I doubt anyone else did."

I huff, turning back to the fire. "I want to help."

"We came up with a plan tonight. Will you come with me to my family's estate and help me handle the reunion with my parents and sisters who think I'm dead?"

There's an edge of nervousness, a vulnerability in his words. I can sense the depth of his request and just how intimidated he is by this plan and his family reunion.

I turn, looking into his eyes that flicker with the reflection of the flames. "As long as I get to spend time with Elisabeth."

He grins. "You two always were getting into all sorts of mischief growing up."

I wave my hand in a circle, pointing at everything around us. "Says the outlaw."

He arches an eyebrow. "And what exactly have I stolen?"

I push down on his shoulder as I stand. He chuckles as I walk away from the fire, back in what I think is the direction of my sleeping hut.

Like the thief that he is, William comes up next to me, looping my arm through his and turning me around. "This way, m'lady."

If only I wasn't afraid to tell him he's already stolen my heart.

Chapter Six
A Rebellious Noble

William Scarlett

My palms rub against my eyelids, but nothing seems to be helping ease the weariness in my bones, and staying awake right now feels impossible. Probably shouldn't have stayed up tending the fire until the wee hours of the morning. But what else was I supposed to do? Every time I closed my eyes, I saw Marian.

In one day, she captured my attention, pulled me into her orbit, and now I'm helpless to be anything except a sphere caught in her gravitational pull.

A sigh escapes me, and I kick the dirt at my feet. Dale doesn't need my help cooking the morning porridge, but if I'm up, I might as well create a semblance of being useful. If anything, sitting on the stump by his cook fire means he's not alone—merry men camaraderie and all that.

Dale eyes me. "She'll probably sleep in, you know."

I shrug. "I'll wait. Robin put me in charge of helping her."

"You glad Little John took over babysitting the prince?"

His question hits hard. Am I glad I'm not with my cousin, Prince Alvor, right now?

A pair of brown eyes and raspberry lips flash in my mind. Yes, yes, I am. Lady Marian is much fairer company.

"Alvor and I worked through the past. It's not his fault his father ordered my death. But I'm glad I'm not delivering the coins from Marian's dowry to Nottingham this morning. Sneaking around with Alvor is impossible; he walks through the forest like a bear."

Dale chuckles. "Robin will teach him."

I scratch the scruff on my cheek. "Will she? Or will they just end up kissing?"

Dale's nose wrinkles, mimicking the look on my face. "What are you and the lady going to be doing today?" he asks, neatly changing the subject.

"Helping you and doing other tasks around camp."

Dale's eyebrows arch. "Good luck with that."

Memories of last night at dinner with Marian have me chuckling. I still can't believe she figured out the camp secret so quickly. She played a simpering courtier well when talking to Alvor and Rowena. I bet they have no clue that she knows. Lady Marian is cunning and overlooked, and I have a feeling she wants it to remain that way.

Movement draws my gaze as a woman approaches the common area of the camp. Familiar rich dark hair flows over one of her shoulders, her peasant dress complementing her figure well.

My heart has been captured, ripped from my chest, and absconded with by Marian. There's no other explanation for why my feet carry me to her without a thought, transfixed by her fingers that deftly weave her scarlet ribbon into her braid.

The urge to reach out and run my fingers through her dark locks catches me by surprise, and I hold myself back.

"Goo—" My voice cracks. I clear my throat. "Good morning, Marian."

She grins shyly. "Morning, William. Though I'm not sure I'd call it good quite yet."

I scratch the back of my neck. "How'd you sleep?"

She winces. "I don't think you want me to answer that."

She ties the ribbon at the bottom of her braid, and I hold out my arm. She loops her arm through mine and rests her hand on my forearm as if we're attending court, the distance between us feeling very formal.

"Care to accompany me this morning, Lady Marian?" I ask.

Her nose wrinkles. "Doing what?"

"First, eating. Then camp chores and preparation for our trip to see my uncle this afternoon."

Her eyes crinkle. "I'm excited to see Elisabeth again. Thank you for inviting me to come with you."

"You're welcome. Now I just need to tell everyone that you're coming."

Her hand tightens on my arm. "Do you think your Robin Hood won't approve?" Her lips quirk, mischief crinkling the corners of her eyes.

I cough to hide my laugh. "Even if Robin didn't, I do. It's my family, and Elisabeth will be delighted to see you."

She sighs, leaning her head on my shoulder as we stroll toward Dale. "I miss Elisabeth. After your father withdrew from court, it was harder to visit her. Occasionally your family would come to the city and she'd visit me. I'd make it to the countryside every few months if I begged Father enough."

I tug on Marian's arm, pulling her tighter into my side. "You? Begging? From what I saw, you have your father wrapped around your little finger."

She smirks. "I'm an only child, of course I do . . . well, did." Her face falls.

I reach up, running my thumb over her knuckles. "Living in the forest won't be forever, Marian."

Her nose wrinkles. "Are you sure?"

I nod.

She stops, looking at my face. Her gaze lands on my lips for a moment before focusing on my eyes. "I'm holding you to that, William Scarlett."

I bow my head. "Anything for you, Lady Marian."

"Red!" Dale shouts. "Get over here."

I straighten. "Duty calls. Want to help?"

Marian smiles. "Might as well earn my keep, right, highwayman?"

I grin. "We'll make an outlaw of you yet, Lady Marian."

For the daughter of a rich duke, Marian works hard. I don't even know if my sisters could do the labor she's done today without complaint. She's scrubbed laundry, easily talked with the women of the camp, peeled and chopped vegetables for Dale, all with a smile gracing her lips.

We've finally sat down for our late midday meal after everyone else has been served. Marian eats with gusto, not once complaining about the thin soup.

"The carrots are good," she murmurs.

I bump her shoulder with mine. "Thanks for cutting them for Dale."

She grins. "I've never peeled or chopped a carrot before, but it was fun. In fact, it felt liberating to wield a knife and feel useful. I don't even care that this is a simple stew, because I'm the one who helped make it."

I nod. "There's something special about eating food you made with your own two hands. It's nice being out here working for my meals and shelter, and providing for others."

Her dark eyes study me. "You know, working and providing for others is what a duke with an estate does, right?"

I squirm, my knee bouncing. "Yes, but I don't know if I'm fit to be a duke anymore. My father is amazing. I'm afraid I've lost all manners since living in the wilderness."

She snorts and covers her mouth. "Excuse me, but that's ridiculous. Granted, you stole a kiss from me before we even came to camp, and a duke wouldn't have done that, but you haven't forgotten your studies; you've just been applying it in your daily life out here."

The memory of Marian's lips on mine flits through my mind for a moment before I focus on the rest of her words. "I'm pretty sure it was a trade, given willingly." Her cheeks flush and I lower my voice, whispering in her ear, "So you're telling me I'm not hopeless?"

Our eyes meet, and the world fades.

"No," she whispers.

Leaves rustle at the edge of the forest, and men's voices snap the tether between us.

Marian leans away, and I turn in time to see Alvor stumble into camp.

Chapter Seven
A Known Secret

Marian

We meet Alvor at the edge of the gathering area.

"Did something happen?" William asks. "Where's Little John?"

Alvor shakes his head, a furrow between his brow. "Nothing happened besides me seeing the horrible life my father has inflicted upon our people." His words are sharp, hurt threading through his tone. "Little John disappeared a while back. Something about horses and finding Row—Robin."

I study his face. I became very familiar with it in the court. His eyes were always a dark blue color. But today—today something has changed in them. Though dark circles betray his tiredness, his eyes, well, they're almost . . . lighter?

"You look different today, Prince Alvor," I comment.

He nods, his lip curling, though his anger doesn't seem to be directed at me. "I should hope so. I'm a completely different person now than I was even a day ago."

I shake my head. "No, it's more than that. Yes, being an outlaw and living with bandits changes you. I mean, my hair is in a simple braid this morning, and I'm having stew for lunch. No. There is more to your changes. Your eyes are brighter." I step closer, looking up into his face, into his eyes. "Your eyes were darker. They've always been blue, but now they're bright, as if filled with light."

I take one last glance at them, their bright blue almost hypnotizing with how they shine. William grabs my hand, looping it through his arm again, and I lean into him, soaking in his comfort as I try to put more pieces of this puzzle together.

Alvor lets out a heavy breath, as if the weight of the world is off his shoulders. "That's probably because my father's cursed magic is gone. Row—Robin used magic to help rid me of the rest of it somehow."

What magic does Rowena have? And does William have magic too? I should ask him, because life has been brighter since we kissed.

How interesting.

I quickly don my courtier persona. "Robin Hood must be very powerful. I'd really like to meet the man, if you can track him down."

Alvor looks past me, his eyes widening before a small smile curls his lips. He spares me a glance. "I'm sure you'll meet Robin Hood eventually, Lady Marian. For now, there's someone I need to talk to." He skirts around us and walks away toward a womanly figure at the far end of the camp.

Someone to talk to? No. Pretty sure he's going to want to go kiss Rowena. That man is in love.

I turn to William, patting his chest. "There are a lot of secrets in this camp, Red. I cannot wait until I unravel them all."

Ugh. His nickname is ridiculous.

William grins. "There are. One day, I'll tell you about all of them."

I sigh, leaning my head on William's shoulder. "Alright, I guess I can be patient."

Why am I still acting besotted with William? Who am I trying to convince, and why? Is it because I think having everyone connect me to William will help keep me safe? Is it because I can't shake the persona I adopted when I was at court?

Because this—this doesn't feel like an act. Not when my highwayman looks down at me with that knowing look. William Scarlett can see through my acting like no one else. How long have I hidden my true self from people? Because right now, I don't think the outlaws are the only ones who hide themselves behind a mask.

Maybe falling for William Scarlett isn't the worst idea I've ever had. Especially when he makes me feel seen and appreciated, despite my efforts to mask who I am.

My gratitude to Little John for finding horses for us to ride to William's estate knows no bounds. This means I won't have to stay another night in a hut, and I might even sleep in an inn tonight, or even better, at Duke Scarlett's home.

Maybe Elisabeth will share her room with me like when we were children, though I don't know if she'd want to stay up giggling with me after knowing I kissed her brother, and I'm never telling her that I want to repeat the experience despite my better judgment.

I stuff my dress and the box of jewelry Little John gave back to me into my saddlebags. I don't mind the camp lifestyle, but I really don't want to come back here. Working with my hands wasn't too bad, but give me embroidery hoops any day and I'll be pleased. Embroidery hoops *and* a real bed.

Definitely a real bed.

William approaches from the side. "Need help mounting?"

I nod my head, biting my lip as I look at the saddle. "Yes, please. I haven't ridden astride in ... ever."

He pats the horse's neck. "You'll be a professional soon enough. I'll stay near you to help if needed."

"Thank you," I whisper.

He runs his hand over the saddle. "I'll lower the stirrup to help you get up and adjust it once you're on."

A nervous laugh escapes me. "I don't know what that means, but I trust you."

He grins. "Mighty dangerous to trust a highwayman, m'lady."

His playful words set my nerves at ease. This banter? I can handle this. "Is it?"

He smirks before stepping behind me. His voice is a whisper, his breath stirring the hairs on the back of my neck. "Put your foot in the stirrup, and when I lift you, swing your other leg over the saddle."

His hands grip my waist, and I have to remind myself to breathe.

I grip the sides of the saddle, lift my leg, and say prayers of thanks to Solwain that I'm wearing a riding skirt one of the women in camp found. The skirt splits down the middle, and the next second I'm weightless, in the air, though seemingly tethered in place by William's grip.

I swing my leg over and settle myself into the saddle. Only then does William let go, though the lingering heat of his touch has yet to fade.

William hands me the reins. "Ready?"

If he's asking if I'm ready to fall for him completely, then I think the answer is yes. But of course, that wasn't really his question.

I lean forward, patting the horse's neck. "As I'll ever be."

And maybe, just maybe, falling for William Scarlett will be the right choice.

CHAPTER EIGHT
A Loving Family

William

I'm the first one off my horse when we get to my uncle's office. Marius, Little John, and Marian stay on their mounts. I don't want to leave Marian behind, but I doubt Robin wants all of us stuffed into a room hearing about magic and breaking curses.

Marius winks when I meet his gaze, the minstrel nodding his head toward Marian. "We'll go find some lodging for the evening and get our guest a meal while you all . . . discuss things."

Marian smiles, a smirk on her lips, before she turns to Marius. "Oh wonderful, I've been meaning to ask you about some of your songs, Marius."

I hold in my groan. It was the wrong thing to tell her about how I don't like ballads. She's been encouraging Marius's minstrel ways our whole trip, and my ears are tired.

Marius laps up the attention as any good performer does. "I'll be happy to play some for you."

Marian grins and urges her horse forward and away from the office. She's become a natural. Riding for hours from the south side of the kingdom up to my family's northern estate was no small feat, and though we'll all be sore tomorrow, she handled the excursion without complaint.

I walk to the door of the building and watch as Little John takes the lead, Marius and Marian behind him as they ride into the village.

When their horses turn a corner, I remember Alvor and Robin, who are supposed to come with me to meet my uncle Standford. They're a few steps away, whispering furiously. I take a moment to study them, noting the way Alvor leans toward her and how Robin lights up in his presence even if she tries to hide it.

Marian is right. They're totally in love.

They finish speaking, and Robin meets my gaze. I smirk, bouncing my eyes between the two love birds, and she blushes.

Ah, our fearless leader. Never thought I'd see the day she fell for a man, though I'm not as surprised as I thought I would be about those two. The few times I remember seeing Robin growing up, she was always hanging around Alvor.

I take a deep breath and open the door to Uncle Standford's clinic. Just as in years gone by, Aunt Marny sits at the front desk with her knitting needles flying.

Warmth fills my chest at the familiar sight.

"Doctor will be right with you," she says, her focus on her project.

I walk over and crouch in front of her desk until I'm at eye level. She pauses and looks up. I can't help the teasing words that slip from my mouth. "Hey, Aunt Marny, guess who's back."

Her eyes go wide as saucers, and I know I've shocked her when her knitting falls from her hands. She reaches across the table, pulling me into a hug. "William, my boy. Oh, how we've worried about you. They said you died, but I couldn't ever believe it. Your parents didn't either. But my boy, why haven't you come home sooner?"

She hugs me tighter, and I find it hard to breathe, but I will not complain, because Aunt Marny's hugs are the best. I haven't had one in too long.

Suddenly, she pushes me away, scowling. "You ridiculous boy, you've been alive this entire time? You couldn't have told any of us where you went?" She smacks the back of my head before hugging me again. "Oh, it's so good to see you."

The door to the back room opens, and Uncle Standford walks out. If there was ever a question of what I'll look like in thirty years, all I need to do is look at my uncle. Red hair still blazing with a hint of white at the temples, crinkles at the corner of my eyes, and hopefully I'll have smile lines like his too.

Except those lines I remember seeing are currently turned down in a frown as he turns to look at us. "Marny, what's all the fuss about?"

I step away from Aunt Marny and hold my arms open wide. "Hello, Uncle."

My uncle's arms squeeze me tight as I give him one last hug. He slaps my shoulder and waves as I mount my horse. It was good to see my aunt and uncle, but now that Robin and Alvor have some answers for how to help the kingdom, it's time to lead us all to my family's home.

The route is second nature as I weave through the thinning buildings. We turn the corner to the last row of buildings. Down the road Marius waves from where he stands holding the reins of the three horses.

Marian and Little John appear from the doorway of the local inn. Marian walks toward my horse and I scramble to dismount.

Talking with my aunt and uncle was healing, but the information we learned about breaking the king's curse on the kingdom has my nerves on edge. Marian's calming presence feels like something I need more than want.

Though I don't know how I feel calm around her when she makes my heart race. I step up next to her, and it's as if my magic, that calming light always glowing in the back of my mind, burns brighter and calmer, soothed by her presence. My magic has already told me how important she is. Now I have to figure out what part she plays in our coup.

Marian holds out a roll, and I intentionally brush my fingers against hers as I take it. We're not officially courting, but I'm not going to sit back without making my intentions known.

Marian's cheeks pink at the gentle touch and she smiles. "How's your uncle?"

"He's good. It was nice to see him and my aunt again. I missed them."

Marius's words to Alvor catch my attention "—we might need to beg for lodging with Red's family."

I turn to the rest of our group. "It should be no problem; there were always plenty of empty rooms growing up, I'm sure we can fit everyone there."

Little John frowns, looking more like a big bear with his stature and grumpy attitude. "Are you sure? I feel having several unannounced guests will become fast spreading gossip, Red."

Gossip? Didn't he realize riding through the town my family rules over would start the rumor mills? I shrug. "We're almost to the end of everything, right? My family and servants can be discreet."

Marian smiles and loops her arm through mine, leaning into my side. "I wouldn't mind sleeping in a real bed."

My blood races at Marian's touch, and I can't help but grin as I look at her hopeful face. Any thoughts of having anyone stay anywhere else besides my family estate are wiped away.

"Then it's decided—we're going home."

We ride into the empty courtyard, the familiar gray walls of the castle with spires topping the four towers welcoming me home. The Scarlett Estates are hundreds of years old, and the weathered stones testify of the care and wealth of generations of ancestors who came before.

Excitement courses through me as I urge my mount to stop. Long have I dreamed of the day when I could hold my mother, tease my sisters, and clap my father on the back, again. It's been so long, and my memory has faded, the memory of their voices distorted with time.

The stable boys, who used to be little kids running around with sticks a few years ago, come and take our horses away.

I approach Marian, who happily loops her arm through mine, easing the lump in my throat. Everything is so familiar, yet different. The castle hasn't changed, but it looks more weathered, and everyone walks about with slumped shoulders, their frames thinner than I remember.

Has the king's greed affected even my father's estate?

Ridiculous question. I know it has. Though we've had few refugees from this far north, I know Father has not been spared from the ridiculous taxes and ire of King Ferdinand.

Marian and I walk across the courtyard together, and suddenly I'm not so worried about seeing my family for the first time again, but rather, how they'll react to seeing Marian on my arm. She's Elisabeth's friend first, but I'm hoping she'll become more to me than just a friend. My body hums, and my fingers twitch at my side, wanting to grip something, but I keep my hand still. No need to grip a weapon while entering my family's home.

My palms sweat. My throat constricts. Is this a reaction to bringing home a lady? Or is this because I'm seeing my family for the first time in years after Robin faked my death?

I wipe my free hand on my trousers.

Both. Definitely both.

The front doors of the castle open, and Brandt, our butler, quakes when he sees me, tears misting over his eyes as he searches for something to say. "Lord William, please follow me to your mother's sitting room. Your family anxiously awaits to see if you are in fact... r-real."

He bows and turns, retreating inside.

My chest constricts, but I force out a chuckle, imagining the look on my family's faces at the news. "This should be entertaining," I murmur to Marian, who squeezes my arm and returns my smile.

I lead us through the entrance hall to the family sitting room, only stopping when my hand grips the handle.

Why is it so hard to breathe?

Marian wraps her arms around my waist, and then suddenly Rowena is hugging my other side too.

Rowena whispers, "You can do this. It's been a long time, but they love you."

I bite my lip, a lump in my throat. A hand clasps my shoulder, and I turn to Marius.

He grins. "This will be a tale I'll happily spread when the time is right. The beautiful reunion of Red the bandit, who sheds the mask of his past to return to the Scarlett Castle in triumph."

Maybe Marius will sing it at my wedding. The thought enables a chuckle to break through the myriad of feelings drowning me.

Rowena pulls away, but when Marian tries to step back, I catch her hand, halting her progress. "Stay," I whisper so only she can hear.

Her cheeks flush, but she nods.

I take a deep breath before opening the doors, moving forward with a feigned confidence into a room I never thought I'd step foot in again.

Mother sees me first. She wraps her arms around my neck and pulls me down into her embrace, peppering my cheeks with kisses. I look over in time to hear Elisabeth squeal as she embraces Marian, the two walking over to sit together on the couch. But in a moment, Elisabeth is at my side, hugging me and laughing.

Father finally makes it through to hug me. He smells exactly the same, like his office, which is full of paper, ink, and his favorite peppermint tea that Mother makes to help with his stress levels.

"I prayed to Solwain every day for you, son," Father murmurs in my ear.

"Thank you," I whisper as a tear trails down my cheek.

Marian catches my eye as she discreetly wipes away the wetness on her cheeks.

And in this moment, I make a promise to myself and Marian.

I will reunite her with her father one day soon, because everyone needs family.

CHAPTER NINE
A Healing Garden

Marian

The garden is in full bloom, though the morning air has an invigo-
rating coolness. It's refreshing to be clean and in a nice dress again,
baths having been the first thing that happened after the reunion last night
between William and his family.

Elisabeth and Georgiana, William's sisters, walk ahead of Rowena and
me, though I don't mind the distance. I've been trying to pay attention to
their conversation but have continually found myself distracted. Not by

the scenery, but rather by thoughts of a certain redhead. I'm grateful I'm walking next to Rowena who seems fine strolling without conversation.

I kick a rock in the pathway before me with the boots I borrowed from Elisabeth, sending it shooting in front of us with an aggression I didn't realize I had within me. Granted, I spent way too much time last night biting my tongue so I wouldn't spill the events of the last few days to Elisabeth.

A yawn threatens to escape me, but I hold it in. There's a thunderstorm raging inside of me, a mess of feelings, political intrigue, and the desire to do something but not knowing what. All leading to the need to kick rocks and yell into the bright blue sky.

Why would Solwain, our great God, and the one who gifted the world with light magic, allow such darkness to inhabit the lands? Why allow his magic to be twisted into curses that destroy families and happiness?

And why do I feel like all I am is a woman who knows how to play a simpering fool? There's nothing for me to do to help with the coup to overthrow the king. I feel useless as everyone plans a way to put Alvor on the throne.

My fingers clench into fists as trilling bird song cuts through the air.

I wish I could mimic the bird's tone, to feel half of its joy. Doubts have plagued me since I awoke. But the fact is, I like William Scarlett. With each interaction, my walls break down around him, but now ... now we're at his estate, surrounded by his family, and I don't know what that means for us.

I'm pretty sure there is an *us*, but maybe I just need to hear the words clearly spoken from him.

It was easy to get caught up in being in the forest, surrounded by outlaws, and having been kissed by a masked highwayman. All of our flirting, well those actions have consequences, and now that we're here and he's been restored to his title, will he still care for me?

I *was* confident in his affections. He's been attentive, and there are quite a few times I've caught him watching me or glancing at my lips. Those are good signs, but what if his family doesn't approve of the match? What if his father has other plans for him as mine did for me?

Rowena clears her throat from where she walks beside me. "May I ask you a question, Lady Marian?"

I turn, looking into the kind woman's face. No man would think she's the rumored bandit Robin Hood if they saw her in the noblewoman's gown she wears with ease, her hair piled on her head, a touch of rouge on her cheeks.

Rowena's smile is small as she spares me a glance before focusing ahead. "Do you care for William Scarlett? Or are you toying with him?"

Only the etiquette training my daddy put me through keeps me from stumbling at her question. "Pardon?"

Rowena stops, turning toward me with the grace and poise of a noblewoman. Her face is serene, not a speck of emotion betraying her, her eyebrows pleasantly arched in question over her hazel eyes. They're greener than mine, which lean more brown. "We are both intelligent women who know more than most men think we do. Be straightforward with me. Are you interested in William Scarlett? Or is he a flirtation for you?"

I tilt my head, studying the serious woman before me. "Why do you care? I've seen your reaction to Prince Alvor. Is he a flirtation for you?"

Rowena winces and clasps her hands against her waist. "No. No, he is not."

We're quiet as we study each other.

"Rowena, may we do away with the secrets? I know you're Robin Hood. I know you've been saving William and others, along with any stray villagers you bring into your fold. You've clearly changed Alvor and preserved the lives of your merry men. Why are you asking me this question? I pose no threat to you, and I doubt you hold feelings for William."

My heart stops when she turns away and walks toward a bench. She sits, patting the empty space beside her. We arrange our skirts, and her hands return to her lap, her knuckles white.

"I figured you might have known more than you let on." She pauses, picking at a thread on her skirt. "I worry for William. He's been like a brother to me since he joined the camp. He asked me the same questions about Alvor just the other day, worried about my heart. I guess I felt the need to protect him and look after him as well."

I shake my head. Could Rowena's magic allow her to read my mind? Does she know of my own doubts concerning William and his affections?

I take a breath. I cannot speak for William, but I can speak for myself. "Rowena, I am no threat to William. I am sure that if anything, I'm a mere flirtation for him. I'd like to be more, but we haven't had time to speak of our relationship. I don't know how much Alvor has said, but I wasn't well liked at court. Probably because of the curse by King Ferdinand, but more likely because I didn't put up with insults and demeaning men. I spent time with Prince Alvor because he was one of the few nice men around."

She grins. "That does sound like Alvor." She pauses, biting her lower lip. "I'm sorry, Marian. I haven't treated you with the respect that you have earned or naturally deserve. I've been petty and jealous. Will you forgive me?"

I reach over, gripping her hands in mine. "Of course I forgive you. You're my future queen, if Alvor has anything to say about it. I want to help you. You've done the hard work for years on your own; it's time to share the burden of saving the kingdom and its people."

Her eyes mist over, but she blinks away the emotion before it spills down her cheeks. "Thank you, Marian."

I bob my head. One problem solved . . . for now.

An idea sparks in my mind, and I reach over and grip her hands again. "Now, what can I do to help this rebellion?"

A sharp glint enters her eyes as her lips tip up. "How influential is your father? We might need some backup in the coming days."

My hope blossoms like a flower. "Oh, I do think he could be quite convinced to do just about anything I say."

Rowena grins. "Wonderful. Let me tell you what you need to know."

CHAPTER TEN
A Meddling Sister

William

Hooves clatter on the cobblestones as I race into the courtyard, hopping off my gelding as a stableboy rushes out to grab the reins I throw his way. My boots pound on the stone as I sprint up to the castle. I throw open the door, running through the halls until I hear noise coming from the music room.

The heavenly notes of a harp ring through the air as Elisabeth sings, the peace at odds with the panic clawing at my chest.

I step into the room, drinking in the sight of Marian, her elegant fingers plucking the strings of the instrument in her lap. Her eyes meet mine, and something of my despair must be written on my face, for she freezes. "William, what's wrong?"

Her question unleashes the flood of emotions I've held back since leaving the capital hours ago. She rushes to me as my knees hit the floor, my hands covering my face as tears stream down my cheeks.

"It's all gone wrong," I choke out. "So wrong."

Marian's cool hands frame my face as she tilts it up, prying at my fingers until I can see her eyes, her gaze steady and calm. "Tell me everything."

I wrap my hands around hers as they frame my face. "Our plan? It's been ruined. The merry men have been captured. I'm the last one left. Father can't leave the castle, nor can the guards we sent with him. Everyone is trapped. Rowena, Alvor, Father. It's all... it's horrible, Marian."

Elisabeth comes over, a glass of water in her hands. "Come, brother, no use crying on the floor. At least move to the settee so we all can languish in sorrow comfortably."

My sister's blasé statement catches me off guard, and so does Marian's quiet giggle. The lightness of the sound contrasts with the despair in my chest, driving away the darkness. She tugs on my hand and I follow her, accepting the water from Elisabeth before sitting next to Marian on the emotional support settee.

Elisabeth brings over a tea tray, and when she pours me a cup, I can't help but murmur, "Can't a man cry to the woman he's wanting to court in peace?"

She arches an eyebrow. "Not when you need a chaperone, and especially not when you haven't gotten permission from her father to court her either."

I glare at my little sister, who unknowingly is spot on for why I haven't asked Marian if I can officially court her yet.

Marian squeezes my hand. "William. What's our plan?"

Her serious tone brings me back to the darkness of our reality. "King Ferdinand had everything figured out. Our entire band has been captured. Everyone is trapped in the castle, and—" I can't get the rest of the words out. The gruesome end planned for my family and friends is too horrible to mention.

"So what are we going to do?"

I turn, looking into Marian's face, determination written across her elegant brow. "What is there to do?"

Marian smirks. "Plan another coup."

I saddle Elisabeth and Marian's horses, then hand each of them a dark cloak normally worn by our guards. It will be a long night riding through the forest to get back to the capital. There are many things we need to put in place, and the clock is ticking.

Elisabeth walks out of the castle first in a simple gown, her hair braided back. For the first time, I take her in, noting her maturity. She looks years older than the image I kept in my mind while I lived in the forest. She's no longer a little girl, but a woman, full grown and ready to gallivant on rebellious missions.

Elisabeth steps over to her horse, and I help her into her saddle. She grips my hand before I step away. "I'm glad you see Marian for her brains, brother. It's about time someone wasn't distracted by her beauty."

I chuckle. "Oh, I'm plenty distracted."

She rolls her eyes and lightly smacks me upside the head. "You are such a man. It's a good thing you're a decent man who appreciates her for who she is, or else we wouldn't be executing her plan, which was much better than yours, might I add."

There are plenty of words that run through my mind at Elisabeth's statement. Assurances that I'm drawn to Marian for more than her looks. I doubt I could write a ballad at the drop of a hat like Marius can. But I no doubt could wax long in my assurances that I'm drawn to Marian because she can outsmart me on any given day; her mind is stunning, her wit captivating, and the way she exudes light all pull me in like a moth to a flame. But none of those things feel right to say to my younger sister. We need to focus on the plan Marian hatched—especially when I hear the light tapping of boots coming across the courtyard.

I turn, staring at the fierce woman approaching me.

Marian stops, her gaze meeting mine, her lips turned up in a sassy smile. "Distracted?"

That sassy mouth that first kissed me in the forest tempts me again. Two can play at this game.

I close the distance between us with two steps, until I'm staring down into Marian's dark eyes. "And if I was?"

Her voice comes out on a quiet breath. "I'd offer you a trade."

My hand comes up, a finger tracing her cheekbone and traveling down to her jaw, tilting her chin higher as my pulse races. "If I were to accept?" I whisper.

She shivers, and my other hand slides beneath her cloak, capturing her waist and pulling her against me. A small gasp escapes her lips, and just as I'm about to taste them, there's a loud, "Ahem," from behind me.

Elisabeth's voice rings out over the quiet courtyard. "And *this* is why you need a chaperone. You are the son of a duke, not a highwayman. You may not kiss my best friend while I'm watching, thank you very much."

I sigh. "Just close your eyes, Elisabeth."

She gasps, outraged. "Absolutely not."

Marian giggles and pulls away, the moment completely ruined. I keep in all of my grumblings about annoying little sisters, but I don't hold back my withering glare. Elisabeth doesn't seem to care; she just smirks and raises her eyebrows. Unfortunately, this will not be the last time I hear about me courting her best friend, though I think she approves of us.

Marian slips her hand into mine, and I lead her to her horse. She groans as she gets into the saddle. "I thought I wouldn't have to ride for a few more days."

I hold her horse steady as she situates herself. "The ride will help loosen your muscles, though I can't deny you'll be sore in the morning.

Her mouth twists in a quick pout before she sighs playfully. "The things we do for our kingdom."

"Indeed," I whisper.

As I mount my horse, I make a promise to myself—I'm not waiting until after we win to kiss Marian again.

CHAPTER ELEVEN
A Bewildered Father

Marian

I have never been so sore in my life. If I don't have to ride a horse ever again, it would still be too soon. Give me a carriage for the rest of my lifetime, thank you.

The back alleyway behind my family's mansion comes into view. Traveling the back roads through the capital was a new experience for me, and I'm grateful William knew where he was going. William enters the alley first, stopping at the servants' entrance. I ride up behind him, Elisabeth at the rear.

William dismounts before helping me down and holding me steady while I find my footing. There is no way I'm walking into my home with the elegance of a noblewoman. I will be hobbling. But I doubt William cares about my gracefulness, not with how attentive he's been on our ride.

Honestly, I had forgotten Elisabeth was even there until it was too late to hide how much her older brother makes me swoon. I will never hear the end of it. But at least the secret is out, and we can talk openly about my interest. There wasn't time as we got ready to ride here, but I imagine she and I will speak of it tonight. Her guest room is near mine, and I foresee a night of warm tea and rehashing everything that's happened over the past few days with the added light of my feelings for her brother.

William walks before us, hand on the hilt of his sword strapped to his side. He knocks on the kitchen door, and a guard opens it.

I push William aside and step into the torchlight. "Sebastian, it's me, Lady Marian. Let us in and send someone to wake my father."

Sebastian nods, ushering us into the dimly lit kitchens, and turns down the hallway to the servants' rooms. Elisabeth and I shed our cloaks, while William stays hooded, as we walk up to the next floor where my father's rooms are. There's shuffling ahead, and Father's door swings open before we reach it.

"Marian?" he whispers.

I dash forward, wrapping my arms around his paunchy waist, and hug him tightly. "Daddy, I'm home."

"Oh . . ." He shakes as he pulls me tightly against him. "My girl. My baby girl. You're here." He pulls back, his hands moving to my face, inspecting me and then my clothes. "They didn't hurt you, did they? Did you marry one of those highwaymen? Those filthy bandits?"

I turn back, looking at my late night companions. "Well, no. I didn't marry any of them—at least not yet."

William steps forward, his hood falling away from his face as his hand slips into mine. He bows his head toward my father. "Hello, Duke Wessex."

If I thought Father was shocked by my appearance, there is no way to describe the pale whiteness that comes over him at seeing William.

Father snaps his fingers. "Jenkins. Get us refreshments. Bring them to the pink room. It's going to be a long evening."

Father's manservant springs to attention, and I lead us to my favorite room in the mansion. I take in the stoked fire, floral paintings adorning the wall, and the pink curtains pulled over the windows. This was my mother's sitting room, and after she passed, my father took up doing most of his business and socializing here. We both spent most of our time here as I grew up. In a way, it feels like I know my mother because of how fondly Father treats this space that she claimed as hers.

Father settles in his wingback chair while William sits between Elisabeth and me.

Father studies William, who has yet to release my hand. He pulls his small flask from his pocket and looks at it, murmuring, "I imagine I'll need this."

Before he's able to take a sip, William leaps forward, grabbing the flask from his hands. "Actually, sir, it'd be better if you were sober."

Father's brow bunches as he looks up at William. William tilts his head, studying my father before placing his hand on Father's shoulder. William's hand starts to glow before the light winks out, but not before I see a mist of darkness floating away from my father and into the shadows behind him.

Father's eyes go wide, and he's utterly still as William returns to his seat beside me. We're silent until Father gathers his faculties. He spears William with his gaze. "What was that?"

"Magic, Your Grace. I just cured you of what little curse was lingering around you from King Ferdinand."

Father splutters. "Curse?"

William nods and explains everything I learned from Rowena about King Ferdinand's curse and what has been transpiring at the castle. Father grows paler, his eyes widening by the minute until I'm not sure if he's going to faint or go into shock.

He grips the lion heads carved into his armrest, his knuckles white. "The king must be stopped," he whispers.

We all nod.

"That's why we came here, Father," I say.

William's fingers squeeze mine. "We have one full day left to make preparations. Everything hinges on the wedding and executions."

Father stares at the mantel. A painting of Mother sits atop it, her kind face overlooking the room. "I shall speak to those who are not stuck at the castle. They must know what has been happening. We shall rally our forces. If King Ferdinand wants a spectacle, we shall give him one."

William bows his head. "There are lives at stake, Your Grace."

Father's eyes meet mine. "More than just lives, young Scarlett. My daughter's happiness is threatened, and I shall not stand for it." Father stands, all weariness gone from his visage. "To bed with you. I have letters to write and plans to make. You all need rest. Elisabeth, I would appreciate if you were to stay with my Marian for the night and be her companion during the day. There is safety in numbers."

Elisabeth nods and loops her arm through mine. "That was our plan as well."

Father bobs his head. "Good, good, good. Young Scarlett, there is a guest bedroom at the *far* end of the hallway. You may use it."

William's eyebrows rise.

Father tsks. "Don't think I missed the subtle foreshadowing of your future with my daughter. I have yet to give my permission, and until then, despite what may have happened in the woods, we shall abide by the laws of propriety in my household."

William bows his head. "Yes, Your Grace."

Father harrumphs and walks out of the room, leaving the rest of us to collect ourselves.

William holds out his elbows. "May I escort you ladies to your room?"

My answer is easy, and I loop my arm through his. His sister's response is less pleasant as she grabs his arm and yanks us toward the door. "Let's go, and if we walk quickly, I may let you sneak a kiss before I lock us in our rooms tonight."

William's eyes go wide for a moment before he shakes off his sister and bends down, his arms sweeping my legs out from under me as he cradles me against his chest. I slap my hand against my mouth to hold in my squeal of surprise, but I can't help the laughter that spills out as William sprints down the hallway with me in his arms.

He reaches my bedroom door with a little guidance, and only then does he let my feet touch the ground. We look back to see Elisabeth moseying down the hallway. She stops in front of the library doors and opens them, winking at me before heading inside.

William's eyes meet mine, a feverish tint to them as he wraps his arm around my waist, his hand coming up and weaving itself into the hair at the nape of my neck.

"May I kiss you?" he whispers.

"Will you give me your name?"

He grins. "I'll give you anything you'll ask for, Lady Scarlett."

Chapter Twelve
A Romantic Trellis

William

The sun still lies beyond the horizon, though the eastern sky begins to grow brighter. The cool wood bites into my palms as I hoist myself off the ground, climbing the trellis to Marian's bedroom window. Luckily, the family rooms are on the second story of the house, so the fall won't be too bad if something were to happen. But I really hope I don't suffer an injury for this foolish idea.

My knuckles rap against the glass of Marian's window. It's foolish to have stayed this long, and I know I'm endangering the household by doing this instead of being on my way. But there is no way I'm heading into the den of a cursed lion without saying goodbye to the woman I love.

A muffled noise sounds on the other side of the glass before the curtains part to reveal . . . my sister.

Elisabeth rolls her eyes and sticks her tongue out before turning back to the room.

A very long moment later, Marian comes to the window, hastily tightening her robe around her as she unlatches the glass pane.

"William," she hisses. "What are you doing?"

I hoist myself up a small step higher so my face is closer to hers. "Saying goodbye to the two most beautiful women in the world."

There's a disbelieving laugh from inside. "Nice try, brother, but I'm not going away so you can kiss your lady love. You already did enough of that last night."

Warmth blossoms in my chest. Elisabeth's detour to the library last night was much appreciated. I'm positive I've never loved my sister more than in those moments she let me steal with Marian last night.

I reach into my pocket and pull out the scarlet ribbons I bought when I slipped away to town while at my family's estate. The silk is cool beneath my fingers, the fabric shimmering as the morning sun breaks across the horizon, the golden glow shining against the fabric. "I got you these," I whisper.

She grins, her fingers brushing against mine as she grabs them. "They're beautiful." She smirks. "Any particular reason why you chose this color?"

"Thought you might appreciate the nuance of the color."

She bites her lip, and I take in her fresh face. The blush on her cheeks, the sparkle in her eye, the way she knew I chose the color scarlet for plenty of reasons that are special to the two of us, all remind me of why I've fallen for this captivating woman.

"I . . ." A lump catches in my throat, and I swallow before starting again. "I don't know what is going to happen today, Marian. But I want you to know—"

Marian presses her fingers against my lips, and I stare into her eyes, the words I was about to say reflected in her gaze.

Her hand moves to my cheek, her thumb tenderly stroking my face. "Tell me when you come back." Her hands move to her hair, which she pulls over her shoulder, the dark strands pooling on the stone windowsill.

My hands tighten on the wooden beams. "Marian, what if...?"

She shakes her head as her fingers deftly weave the ribbon into her braid. "No. You will fight to come back to me. I will not let this be our goodbye." She ties the end with a small bow and reaches for my face, her hands cupping my cheeks. "I told my father I'd marry a highwayman. You better not make me break that promise." She leans forward, her lips brushing against mine. "Come back to me?"

"I'll come back tonight if I can."

Elisabeth steps up to the window. "Be safe, brother."

I grab the end of Marian's braid and place a kiss on the ribbon before climbing down the trellis. My horse nickers and I mount, moving toward the entrance into the city. My heart tugs at me and I turn back.

There, standing vigil in the window, are two of the most important women in my life. My resolve hardens into steel. I will see them tonight, if all goes according to plan.

I slip through the walls around the back of the castle and slink through the gardens. The sun moves across the horizon as I study guard rotations and the layout of the palace.

It's the dinner hour, and I know King Ferdinand is occupied. There is no chance of freeing Robin. She's locked in the queen's quarters at the top of the castle, so I focus on rescuing the merry men. The dungeons are at the base of the tower, small windows allowing light in but giving no chance of escape to the inhabitants.

I count to thirty after a round of guards pass by my hiding place in the gardens. I have a few minutes before the next guards walk past here.

The rough bark scrapes against my hands as I push off the tree. I crouch, staying low to the ground as I cross the walkway to the bottom of the tower. I creep along the edge of the stone wall until I find the first window into the dungeons. I drop to the ground, looking into the grate, the darkness beyond overwhelming, along with the stench.

"Little John," I hiss.

There's an answering grunt. "Get out of here, Red. It's a trap."

"No. There must be a way to get you out."

Hands reach up, wrapping around the bars as Little John's face comes into focus. "That's how Much and Stue got stuck down here. Now RUN!"

I grip Little John's hands. "I. Am. Not. Leaving. You."

Little John groans. "You don't understand, Red. The guards in here know you're out there. They just sent someone to get you. Run. Away. Now."

My heart stops and cold washes over me. I hop to my feet, racing toward the trees.

But it's too late.

Chain mail clinks, and the ringing of metal swords leaving their sheaths permeates the quiet garden.

I'm encircled by castle guards.

The captain steps forward, his sword pointed at my chest. "Surrender or die."

Brown eyes flash in my mind, soft lips, and a scarlet ribbon woven through dark hair.

I hold my hands up.

Chapter Thirteen
A Hasty Plan

Marian

The grandfather clock in Father's study chimes the late hour, and still there is no sign of William.

"Father, surely you can send someone out to find him?"

Father doesn't even look up at my request. His reading glasses perch on his nose as he stares at the letters in his hand, their words illuminated by the candlelight. "No. He knew the risk today if he was to accomplish all he had planned. Now, we wait for tomorrow."

"But Father, the king plans on—"

Father's papers crinkle as he moves them down so our eyes meet. "I know. But we won't let him. I've talked to enough nobles today that we will make sure it doesn't happen, dearest. I can't say I'm pleased to know the man courting my daughter was an outlaw for three years, but the fact he's Duke Scarlett's son will redeem him for now."

I lean my chin on my hands as I stare at the fire in the grate. "I would marry him even if he was only a highwayman."

Father tsks. "I will thank Solwain daily that William Scarlett is more than just an outlaw."

"Maybe I should pray."

Father shrugs. "Praying may help. Solwain favors those who are faithful to his goodness, according to what I've read. Though we don't have magic in our family, I don't doubt Solwain may smile upon those he wishes, if they do as he pleases."

A sigh escapes me. "William has magic."

Father chuckles. "I am well aware. That shock he gave me the other night was quite unexpected. But I can think clearer now than ever. I don't know what his magic is, but I am grateful for it."

I lean back, fingering the ribbons in my braid. It's freeing to wear my hair down, rather than in the updos demanded by King Ferdinand.

Being with William feels freeing.

Solwain, please help our people be freed of this wretched darkness.

Elisabeth is sound asleep as I slip out of the covers, grabbing my robe before padding over to the window. The sun crests the horizon, and as I open the glass, a small breeze sweeps through my hair and into the room. I gather the loose strands. The ribbon slips out, and I relish the feel of its silk as I pull it through my fingers.

The calm of the morning is deceptive.

If William has been captured, then he'll be sentenced to death like the rest of the merry men. Today, I'm going to rescue them.

I go to my closet, finding the servant's dress I pilfered from the housekeeper's supplies yesterday afternoon. If Elisabeth knew I was sneaking out this morning, she'd stop me, which is why I move as quietly as possible. She's a sound sleeper, a trait I'm grateful for.

I slip on the plain gown, relishing how easy it is to dress myself with the laces at my side and the simple fabric folds.

Maybe when Rowena is queen, she'll change our fashion for the better. I can't imagine she enjoys the layers of opulent clothing popular among the nobility.

I part my hair down the middle, plaiting both sides before wrapping them around my head like I've seen many maids do. The ribbon ties them together and keeps them in place.

With one last look in the mirror at my altered appearance, I slip out of my room. The manor is quiet, but I'm not surprised. Everyone knows the severity of what is going to happen today.

Father's room is empty even at this early hour. It's expected, as the nobles were instructed to meet at the chapel by the castle this morning. I sigh. One less person to sneak by.

The kitchen is bustling when I step inside, so nobody pays attention as I grab an empty basket and a roll from the breakfast table and head out of the servants' exit.

The footpath out of our meager lands is easy to follow. For once, I'm glad we don't have a sprawling estate; Father's investments with the merchants make up most of our wealth. When I get to the edge of the gate leading into the city, my feet freeze. I've never walked around the capital by myself before. I try to pull up the mental map I have from my visits in that area. At least the king's chapel is easy to find.

My fingers tap against the wood of the gate before gripping it and pulling it open.

A group of women catches my eye. They're walking up the road to the capital, so I slip out, closing the gate behind me, and hurry to catch up with them. I meld with the back of the group, smiling at a woman who glances back at me. Her returning smile doesn't reach her eyes.

The walk into the heart of capital is silent, allowing me time to formulate a plan.

Whispers of gallows, forced marriage, and death was the talk of the servants yesterday. As one woman, I'm not sure what I can do, but my first goal will be to prevent William's death. Then I can focus on helping Rowena.

It's a twenty-minute walk from my estate to the king's designated chapel. Time passes quickly, and we soon reach the courtyard before I'm fully prepared, a plan in place. The women in front of me melt into the crowd. I can barely see over the crush of humans vying for a place to watch King Ferdinand's impromptu wedding and his wicked commands.

I can't see the chapel steps, but it's very clear where William is. At the side of the courtyard is a large set of gallows. My heart stops as I take in the trapdoor he's standing upon, the rope around his neck, and the other merry men from Rowena's camp lined up next to him.

My stomach heaves, and I turn away, losing the roll I ate on the way here.

An old man hands me a handkerchief, and I wipe my mouth. "It's a grim business this morning, ain't it, lassie?"

"'Tis indeed," I whisper.

His wisened brow draws together. "Go home, lass. You do not have to witness this."

I shake my head. "I can't—for I've fallen for one of those outlaws."

His lips thin, his wrinkles more pronounced. "Then you best be sayin' goodbye." He takes my hand and leads me through the crowd to the back of the gallows where a small crowd has gathered. The old man taps my hand. "Best blow him a kiss, lassie," he says before slipping into the crowd.

I wish I could blow a kiss to William, but he's faced away from me, toward the chapel. If I did blow him a kiss, it'd only draw attention, especially if I called out his name. But, oh, how I want to.

The clopping of horse hooves and the sounds of a carriage silence the murmurs of the crowd. We watch as it pulls into the courtyard, and I catch a glimpse of Rowena and King Ferdinand.

Rowena looks beautiful and miserable.

I force myself to put on my carefully practiced mask of neutrality. No one must know that on the inside I'm scheming. My body is utterly still as I face the chapel, but I let my eyes wander, studying the wooden contraption before me.

These gallows were poorly built, with barely any space beneath them for the men to fall. The ropes are tied around each man's neck and are thrown over the top beam, before being tied down to the platform at the back.

If I really wanted to foil King Ferdinand's plan, all I'd need to do was make sure the ropes will not stay taut. Each rope has four woven strands twisted together. My mind hums as pieces click together, a plan forming. If two or three strands are cut, it'll weaken the rope, and if, by some horrible chance, the trap doors are loosed, the ropes won't be able to hold the full weight of William and the merry men.

If only I had a knife.

My eyes dart to the side, looking around for someone who might have a knife within easy reach. I am by no means a pickpocket, but there's nothing like imminent danger to motivate me to try my hand at some lawbreaking skills.

A guard walks by, a sword on one side of his belt and a dagger on the other.

My stomach tightens. I am not a pickpocket, so what can I do instead? Stumble into him and flirt my way out of it while conveniently getting his knife?

That could work.

And if he catches me holding the knife, I'll just flirt more.

Foolproof.

I wipe my palms on my skirt and lick my lips before stepping toward the end of the gallows where two guards stand. When they're within falling reach, I fake tripping.

Almost too easily, my hands land on the waist of a guard. My hands grip the dagger, and as he's stumbling away, I pull it free, tucking it up my sleeve.

"I... I'm sorry, sir."

The guard turns, a frown on his face until he sees me.

I stare up at his grumpy face, forcing a besotted look as I flutter my eyelashes. "I must have tripped. I'm so sorry for stumbling into you, sir."

The transformation on his face is immediate. Gone is his frown as a condescending smile overtakes his face, his gaze roving my body. "No harm done, miss." His eyes meet mine again. "Care to meet up at a tavern this evening?"

I duck my head and force myself not to gag. I tighten my grip on the dagger, moving my hands behind my back as I rock on my heels, playing the innocent maiden. My eyelashes flutter as I look up into his gaze again. "It depends on how . . ." I flit my eyes toward the gallows, only to see a pair of bright blue eyes staring at me.

The guard chuckles. "I understand. This may not be for someone of such . . . delicate sensibilities."

I titter, "You are probably right." I take a step back. "I should . . . find somewhere else to be."

The guard nods. "I'll be at the tavern by the Boar's Inn this evening, miss. If you care to join me."

"We shall see," I murmur. The second guard, who had been half watching our conversation, elbows his comrade, who turns back to the crowd of onlookers.

A sudden gasp rings out from the people around us. I squash the desire to see what's happening; I have no time to waste. I slip up behind the gallows, dagger in hand. Little John's rope is first.

I saw through two strands of his rope before moving on. Marius is next, and I cut three strands. Gasps sound out around me, enough to know that it's not what I'm doing that is catching their attention, but rather the enraged yelling coming from King Ferdinand by the chapel doors.

"Halt!" This shout comes from ahead of me, and I look up to see a guard scowling as he stalks in my direction, a dagger in hand.

There are four more ropes to cut, and I'm finally at William's. My hands move faster, sawing back and forth across the strands until, with a desperate cry, the third and fourth strands snap.

There's a growl from atop the gallows and William comes racing across the platform. His hands are tied behind his back, the rope attached to his noose trailing behind him. He jumps off the platform, his feet hitting the chest plate of the approaching guard before they both land on the ground. William scrambles to pin the man down, using his legs to keep the guard immobile.

I race forward and grip the ropes around William's wrist, sawing through his bindings, my pulse racing with each severed strand. When I'm almost done, William yanks his wrists apart, snapping the remaining frayed strands before pulling the noose from around his neck. He pulls the sword from the guard's sheath, hitting the guard on the head with the handle, knocking the man unconscious.

William looks at me. "Run," he murmurs before facing off with a new set of guards racing toward him. Chaos erupts around us.

I plunge into the crowd. Shouts sound behind me, the stomping of boots dogging my footsteps. Confusion lines the faces of the townsfolk I pass. Elbows hit my sides, and I'm sure I'll be bruised by the end of this foray. People have flocked to the morning's spectacle, and the streets leading from the courtyard are clogged.

After pushing through the last of the crowd, I'm met with an empty street. I race to the edges and turn into the first alleyway I can. I hide behind a stack of crates, slowing my breathing.

The clattering of hooves on the street catches my attention, and I hold my breath as the horse stops at the entryway of my hiding place.

I dare not peek or even move.

Leather creaks, and then I hear soft footsteps.

I lean against the stones of the building behind me, trying to make myself as small as possible.

It doesn't work, because the man steps around the crates.

His red hair catches my eye first, and then I drink in the rest of his face. My highwayman approaches with the speedy stealth of the thief that he is, his smile growing as he closes the distance between us.

William places his hands on the wall on either side of me, and my hands come up to wrap around his neck.

"Who's the outlaw now?" he whispers.

Chapter Fourteen
A Romantic Rendezvous

William

I may have been about to hang, but the moment I felt real fear was when that guard came after Marian. Gratefully, Rowena and Alvor broke the curse soon after I began fighting, which made following Marian easy.

There's no one coming after us, and the weight of the past few years has lifted off my shoulders.

I have Marian trapped between me and the wall, but I'm not going to let on that without having been fed for a whole day, I'm feeling weak, and the wall is helping hold me up. That was a lot of activity on an empty stomach.

Marian smiles as if she hadn't scared years off my life a few moments ago, going against the guard's orders and trying to rescue me. My little outlaw, though if she keeps flirting with me like this, I don't think I'll mind her escapades much longer. Especially because she's using her real smile on me, not that saturnine one she used on that guard—whom I do not like.

"What type of outlaw?" Marian whispers.

"If anyone should be considered a highwayman, it's you, my dear Marian. You've run away with my heart, tied it up in those scarlet ribbons of yours, and now I'm helpless to do anything but fall at your feet, begging for even a moment of your attention."

Her fingers twine in my hair as she brings my face closer to hers. "I think I can spare a few moments, maybe even a few days for you."

One hand drops from the wall, hooking around her waist as I pull her against me. I hold her for a moment, savoring the tender embrace as I bury my nose in her hair, which has fallen out of its braids, the strands and ribbons loose around her shoulders.

Holding her finally calms my racing heart, and as I breathe her in, my pulse settles. "I was so scared for you, Marian."

She hums an indignant sound before her lips brush a kiss on my cheek. "I can handle myself."

"I know," I whisper as I take her mouth with mine, pouring out all the sweet relief of holding her in my arms. The words left unsaid yesterday swirl around us in the gentle caresses and the swooping butterflies fluttering in my chest.

My magic flares with visions of warmth, love, and a life of dedication to our kingdom and each other flashing in my mind's eye. The visions coalesce into one last flash of discernment branded on my heart. Marian is my forever, the one chosen for me by Solwain.

I pull back from our kiss to study Marian's face in this precious moment, and I can't help but laugh when she pouts and leans up, trying to kiss me again.

But hoofbeats from the road distract me, and I turn when a horse makes its way around the crates.

The outraged gasp doesn't surprise me when I see who has caught us in our romantic rendezvous.

"I fight for your freedom, young Scarlett, and this is how you repay me?"

I step away from Marian and shield her from the view of Duke Wessex, whose outrage could kill me where I stand. His reddened face, folded arms, and eyes glaring daggers at me would normally intimidate me for a second, but I've had enough death threats for one day.

So, I bow my head and put on my most winsome smile. "Hello, Duke Wessex."

He narrows his eyes. "A highwayman indeed. Did you kiss my daughter in that cursed forest where you kept her captive?"

"Actually, Your Grace, your daughter kissed me first."

Marian groans behind me as Duke Wessex's jaw drops open, then shuts.

After a moment, the man seems to gather his wits and furrows his brow as he glares at me. "Marian, you shall marry this scoundrel of a future duke immediately. I shall not have your reputation sullied by the knowledge you lived in a forest with this man, unsupervised. Who knows what happened?!"

Marian's hand lands on my arm, and she nudges me to the side until she's facing her father. "Daddy, I already told you nothing happened. We kissed. So what? People kiss each other all the time at court without consequence."

Duke Wessex's face reddens until he reminds me of a ripe tomato. "Kissed? You look as if you've done more than kissing, young lady. Your hair is an absolute disaster."

She folds her arms. "Yes, *Father*. All we did was kiss, and you cannot force William to marry me. Don't you remember what happened last time you tried to force me to marry someone?"

The duke harrumphs and dismounts. I lean over, whispering in Marian's ear, "Um, I would rather you not try to marry any other highwayman besides me, dearest. I don't mind if he forces me to put a ring on your finger."

She smirks and gently smacks my chest. "It's the principle of the thing, William."

I shrug. "Who cares about principle if I get to marry you?"

She glares, but then I'm distracted by the duke stalking toward me. He stops in front of me and pokes my chest as he glares and speaks with a low, menacing tone. "You will court her properly, marry her speedily, and then you will treat her as the noblewoman she is."

At least now Duke Wessex is showing some backbone, and I actually approve of his demands.

So I turn and look into the beautiful brown eyes beside me. "I will do whatever your daughter wishes, Your Grace."

Marian tilts her head and taps her chin before grinning. "I agree with Father's pronouncement. How do you feel about getting married tomorrow?"

I grin. "As long as we can get my family here, I have no complaints."

She pats my chest. "Good. Now let's go home. I'm sure Elisabeth is beside herself with worry, and I have a wedding to plan."

Duke Wessex steps back, shock written across his face as Marian steps around him. We walk to the road where we find Duke Wessex's guards awaiting him. They seem less surprised when Marian demands a horse, and they quickly fulfill her request.

I help Marian mount her horse before hopping back on the one I borrowed from the king's guards.

Borrowed might be a stretch.

Marian turns in the saddle, smiling back at me. "Are you coming?"

I urge my horse forward until I'm next to my future bride. I take her in, messy hair, wide smile, and an inner glow shining forth. "I'll follow you anywhere, Lady Scarlett."

Did you enjoy *Lady Scarlett* and want to read Rowena and Alvor's story? Don't forget to read *Fairest Hunter*!

Want to know what is happening in the rest of the Kingdoms of Miraveil? The series continues with Book 2: *Charmed Beast* – A Retelling of Cinderella and Beauty and the Beast. Find the special editions HERE on Kickstarter.

Author's Note

This book came about after one of my beta readers asked me if William and Marian were getting their own story. My automatic answer was no.

But as most stories do, they start with a small spark and simmer until the words are begging to be released.

As I contemplated what William and Marian's story could be based on, to fall into the retelling sphere, I couldn't help but think of one of my favorite books, *The Highwayman of Tanglewood* by Marcia Lynn McClure. I absolutely adored it, and as I thought of William being a bandit, I began to change it to "highwayman" in my head.

So then I went down a rabbit hole of research, wondering if Marcia had based her book on anything specific.

That's when I found the poem "The Highwayman" by Alfred Noyes.

Reader, I am not a huge fan of poetry. It's not my jam. I especially don't like poems where characters die. But the imagery of this poem wouldn't leave my mind. I suddenly started thinking of Marian, with dark hair and scarlet ribbons, and William and his highwayman mask.

And then the words came.

William and Marian took on a life of their own, and I'm so glad they did. I'm also thrilled that I could write a happy ending for this highwayman. I hope you enjoyed the small tidbits of the original poem woven into the story.

Also by M.K. Felix

The Favored's Curse

Fairest Hunter

Lady Scarlett

(A Companion Novella to Fairest Hunter)

Charmed Beast

Hidden Royal (2027)

Acknowledgements

The biggest thanks for this little book goes to my beta readers who asked for it, and my husband, Carson, who helped make this story way better than it first was.

Carson is my biggest supporter, and I love when he reads my books. It's entertaining for both of us. I'm grateful for his insights, his ability to help me with my characters, and all the things. Can't wait until we actually write a book together.

Of course, I cannot forget my Heavenly Father, who gives me all the inspiration for my stories and helps me write them when my brain feels like mush at the end of the day.

About the author

M.K. Felix writes clean, magical stories where fairy tales get fresh twists, romance stays swoony but sweet, and light always wins in the end. A life-long book lover, she finally gave in to the call of storytelling three years ago and hasn't stopped writing since—especially tales where magic is rooted in light, inspired by her faith and her desire to share the light of Christ with the world.

When she's not twisting fairytales together, you'll find her chasing her two kids, laughing with her husband, or at church, recharging her soul. As a member of The Church of Jesus Christ of Latter-Day Saints, she writes with the hope of bringing wonder, faith, and hope to her readers.

With a bachelor's in Business Management and an associate degree in Project Management, she knows how to wrangle both spreadsheets and plot twists—but she'd always rather be in a world of enchanted forests, cursed princes, and rebels with a cause.

Sign up for M.K. Felix's Newsletter here:

Follow M.K. Felix on Instagram here: